The Adventures of Enrique in Panama

(English and black/white version)

Nayka Barrios Jaén

English translation by:
Diana Catalina Herrera Infante

Illustrated by:
Sarah Fullerton-Barrios, Florida State University
Keke Cartoon - José García, Panama
Juan Sánchez, Panama
Digital Graphic Designer - Mayvi Espinosa, Panama

Dedication

I proudly dedicate this book to Panama, my beloved homeland.

To my mother Dilsa and my grandmother Frede

To all the "Enriques" in my family, including my father

To my grandmother "Flor" and aunt "Lily"

To my stepfather and friend "Beto"

To my uncle "Danilo" and the rest of the family who inspired the names and characters in this story.

Table of Contents

Acknowledgments

First and foremost, thank you to My Generation of Polyglots writers' group.

My class of 2025 at Shorecrest Preparatory School for your enthusiasm this year, for reading with me, and for giving your constructive comments. We had fun!

To my friends and beta readers, thank you for your support, constructive criticism, and encouragement throughout the development of this book:

- To my brother, Panamanian professor of folklore, Carlos Enrique Barrios Jaén, for sharing his practical advice.

- To Belén Johnson from Shorecrest Preparatory School, a national of Andalusia, for sharing her local knowledge.

- To my fairy godmothers and dear friends from Polk State College: Thelma Chicas, Rosalinda Collins, Lisa Gibilisco Rosa, and Arlene Torres.

- To my husband Peter for patiently listening and for brainstorming ideas in this writing adventure.

- To our family friend and world traveler John Kayser.

- To published author and friend Jerry McAbee for giving me his sage editorial advice.

These are the most frequently used words in the story.

Let's make predictions!

1

Preamble

At the end of class, the teacher distributes the **flyer**[1] to all students and says:

—"Here is more information for an adventure next summer."

Enrique is quick to respond.

—"Great! I'm going to talk to my family about the Exchange Program!"

---

1 **flyer** - volante

1 — Enrique

At Enrique's house, everyone gets up early for work and school.

—"Enrique, it's time to go to school," says his mother.

—**"I'm ready![1]"** Enrique replies, and they leave for school.

Enrique is a 17-year-old boy, handsome, intelligent, and athletic. He loves soccer and outdoor activities. He likes science and mathematics, so he wants to go to college to study engineering. Enrique likes his school very much; it is an International School.

His first class of the day is Spanish and Latin American history. The teacher, who is a native of Panama, is one of his favorite teachers.

—"Today we are going to start a new lesson," says the teacher while walking to the map. It will be a lesson on tales and legends of the Indigenous people of a region of Panama, and we will also learn how they maintain their traditions in today's world.

---

1 **I am ready!** - ¡Estoy listo!

—**"How Cool!"**[2] Enrique says. He and the rest of the class remain attentive. The teacher notices the interest and continues talking.

—"Let's start with Panama, my home country," says the teacher. "Where on August 15, 1519, Spain established the first Spanish city called Panama City in the Americas. This city still exists today and is the oldest city on the **Mainland**[3]. The first explorers called it Panama, "The Door of the Seas and the Key to the Universe."

—"Wow!" another student says— "that's the place where the Panama Canal is, isn't it?"

—"Yes, that's right!" says the teacher with a smile. "Panama is a **narrow piece of land**[4], known as an isthmus that connects North and South America and has coasts on two oceans, the Atlantic and the Pacific. You can travel through, or alongside, the Panama Canal by boat, car or train; the distance is 50 miles (80.47 kilometers) ..."

—"What a great idea!" says Enrique. "To go in less than an hour from one ocean to the other, that´s cool!"

—The teacher continues, "My country is small but very beautiful, with **a lot of**[5] history, and you can do numerous outdoor activities. Class! To top it off, there are very interesting mountains, especially a mountain near a valley with a very old legend. That mountain is called *"La India Dormida"* some people say it is **enchanted**[6] by a beautiful Indigenous princess."

This information excites the class, especially the boys.

—"Interesting!" says another boy.

---

2 **How cool!** - ¡Qué guay!
3 **Mainland** - Tierra firme
4 **narrow piece of land** - istmo estrecho
5 **a lot of** – mucho(a)/s
6 **enchanted** - encantados

The bell rings and the class finishes. The teacher **reminds**[7] them:

—"Boys and girls! Talk to your parents about Panama and the flyer about this summer's Exchange Program between Spain and Panama. If they accept, then you can go to Panama."

Enrique approaches the teacher, interested in the lesson, and says:

—"My family is part of Panama's history and I would really like to visit."

She appreciates the comment and with a smile reminds him to talk to his parents about the Exchange Program flyer.

---

7 **reminds** – ella les recuerda

2 — Nice People!

Enrique´s immediate family is small, just three people, Enrique and his parents. Enrique's parents are Spanish; the members of his family are descendants of a **landowner**[1] who received his land and his noble title of Duke, for working as an explorer for the Catholic King and Queen of Spain, Fernando and Isabel, around the year 1492.

Enrique and his parents have their **own business**[2]. It is a **farm of sunflowers**[3]. These yellow flowers are pretty, easy to cultivate, and very popular, because during the day **they turn**[4] to look for sunlight. In the countryside they cut the flowers and sell them. They **also**[5] sell the flowers' **seeds**[6] and the **oil**[7]. Tourists especially like to see these beautiful flowers.

---

1 **landowners** - terratenientes
2 **own business** - negocio propio
3 **farm of sunflowers** – granja de girasoles
4 **they turn** - giran
5 **also** - también
6 **seeds** - semillas
7 **oil** - aceite

During the week Enrique goes to school and on weekends he helps his parents in the sunflower business. Now it is Saturday morning, and Enrique talks to his father.

—"Father, are you going to need help in the sunflower field or the store today?" Enrique asks.

—"Yes, your mother is going to need help in the store, it's going to be a busy morning with the tourists."

In the afternoon, Enrique finishes helping his mother at the store and later goes to play a game of soccer with his friends. He has several friends and among them a best friend or BFF (*Best Friends Forever*), his name is Edilberto Barahona. Edilberto thinks his name is too long, so his parents and friends call him by his **nickname**[8] Beto. He is also Spanish, and they have both attended the same school since first grade.

Enrique and Beto love to eat **snacks**[9] and play video games after their soccer games. The boys also talk about the possibility of traveling to Panama and having their first adventure **without**[10] large school groups, their parents or chaperones.

Enrique says to Beto "I talked to my parents about the cultural exchange."

—"Tell me, what they said?" Beto asks.

—"They said yes... I can go!" Enrique says.

—"That is great!" says Beto. "My parents said yes, too."

—"Great! We're going to Panama!" They both shout for joy, "¡Olé, olé, olé, olé! ¡Panamá, Panamá!"

—"We have the best parents in the world!" says Enrique.

---

8 **nickname** - apodo
9 **snack** - merienda
10 **without** - sin

It's obvious that Enrique and Beto's parents **support**[11] him. They love that Enrique and Beto are friends. Their mothers are good friends too. They are going to coordinate the details of the cultural exchange trip between Spain and Panama that the boys want to experience.

---

11 **support** – ellos apoyan

3 — The exchange almost[1] begins!

There are only four days left of classes, Enrique and Beto are **very excited**[2] because they are going to Panama on August 1st. One of their classes is Design Entrepreneurship and Innovation (DEI). In this class the students learn how to organize the end of the year projects called **"Capstone projects"**[3].

These are very important projects because they are used to help improve or create solutions to a problem in society. At the end of 12th grade, the kids have to complete their projects. They are enthusiastic, but they know that they need to work hard to prepare their projects.

But Enrique and Beto don't want to talk about school projects. For now, they just want to talk about their exchange trip to Panama. The boys have already contacted the families that will

---

1 **casi** - almost
2 **very excited** – muy emocionados
3 **Capstone project** - proyecto final

host them in Panama to ask about the weather because they need to know what type of clothes they should pack in their suitcases.

—"We should wear comfortable clothes because Panama has tropical weather. It is very hot and very humid!" Enrique says.

—"He explains that Panama has two climatic seasons during the year; the **rainy season**[4] goes from April to November, and the **dry season**[5] goes from December to March." Beto reads this information from a Google search on his cellular phone.

They talk more and Beto says, "I'm a little nervous about our trip, I have never traveled by airplane, I always travel by train in **RENFE**[6]!"

—"Do not worry about it! It's okay! Beto. It's a long trip, and you can get plenty of sleep. You can also bring your phone and play video games," Enrique responds.

—"Enrique, are we going to have signal and mobile data on our phones during the flight?" asks Beto.

—"Yes, we are going to have signal and mobile data on our new smartphones, because my mother says she talked to your mother, and they are going to give us two mobiles with international connection," Enrique assures.

—"Perfect! Then we will have internet connection on our trip and in Panama. Super! Our mothers are so smart, they think of everything!" Beto comments.

—"**Of course!**[7] This way, we will communicate daily when we are separated in Panama."

---

4 **rainy season** - estación lluviosa
5 **dry season** - estación seca
6 **RENFE** - La Red Nacional de Ferrocarriles Españoles (RENFE) is the train system that connects Spain's main cities with Madrid, and it has Alta Velocidad (AVE) high speed trains.
7 **Of course!** - ¡Por supuesto!

4 — The Arrival

It is the first of August, and it is the rainy season in Panama. The airplane, in **which**[1] Enrique and Beto travel, arrives at Panama City's Tocumen International Airport. This is a very busy airport that connects many **flights**[2] from a lot of countries around the world with more than one hundred flights a day. It is summer in the north of the American continent and in Europe. It is also high season for tourism, so many people have time off and visit Panama.

The boys get out of the airplane, walk and talk:

—"Enrique, this airport is huge" Beto says, a little **overwhelmed**[3] by the noise. And at that moment, Beto sees his **host family**[4]. It's a couple with a little boy with a **paper sign**[5] that says "Beto". Beto sees the sign and approaches his host

---

1 **which** - el cual
2 **flights** - vuelos
3 **overwhelmed** - abrumado
4 **host family** – familia anfitriona
5 **paper sign** - cartel

family. He greets them as they usually do in Spain, with a kiss on each cheek and hugs them; he is very happy to meet them in person. Beto says goodbye to Enrique.

—"Goodbye! Talk to you soon on the cellphone." Then he walks with his host family to the parking lot, and they leave in a car.

Instead, Enrique looks through the **crowd**[6] and does not see a sign with his name on it, nor his host family either. He is a little worried and confused. A few minutes later, he looks towards the airport gate and sees a very pretty girl looking at him in the crowd. She has a paper sign that says "Enrique." The girl looks very pretty and she appears to be about his age. He is **relieved**[7] and his **heart beats**[8] very fast as he walks up and talks to her.

They talk and introduce themselves, "Good afternoon, my name is Lily, and I am the daughter of your host family."

— Enrique is very happy and says, "Hi Lily, thank you for coming!"

—"I'm going to take you to our house. My mom doesn't drive her car in the city because she is **afraid**[9] to drive in Panama's traffic. There are too many cars in this crazy little city!" Lily explains.

—"**Oh, my goodness!**[10] Well, Lily, you came for me at a good time. You are right, in the Internet search I saw that there is a lot of traffic and also that it is hot and humid in Panama!"

---

6 **crowd** – muchedumbre, muchas personas
7 **relieved** - aliviado
8 **heart beats** – corazón palpita
9 **afraid** - miedo
10 **Oh, my goodness!** – ¡Santo cielo!

—"Enrique, you look very tired," says Lily. "Let's get on our way, so you can meet my parents in person. My mom and dad, Rosa and Danilo, are very nice and **hospitable**[11]."

---

11 **hospitable** - hospitalarios

5 — The Lucky Penny in the Parking Lot

In the airport parking lot Enrique walks with Lily to the car. Lily's car has a sticker with the **Uber**[1] logo on it. Enrique is confused because he has never taken an *Uber* **before**[2].

Suddenly[3], he sees a very shiny copper coin in the parking lot. Enrique learned in his English class about the *lucky penny*. He knows that if he sees a penny on the ground, he should pick it up and put it in his pocket to attract good luck. When he touches it, he feels an unusual energy going through his body, but he thinks **he is just tired**[4] from the trip, so he puts the penny in his pocket.

Enrique and Lily leave the airport; she drives the car. There is a lot of traffic in Panama, but Lily looks very calm as she drives. She is a very nice girl. He wants to talk to her, but doesn't know what to say. He **takes out**[5] the penny of his pocket, looks at it, and thinks it is very shiny. Enrique talks to Lily about the penny.

—"Tell me, Lily, whose face is on the coin? It's different from the face on the Spanish penny."

---

1 **Uber** - Uber is a transportation company with an app that allows passengers to have a ride for a fee.
2 **before** - antes
3 **suddenly** - de repente
4 **he is just tired** – él solo está cansado
5 **takes out** - saca

—"In Panama, the pennies are made of **copper**[6]. The face on the penny is of the *Indio Urracá* who was an Indigenous leader who resisted Spanish colonization," Lily responds.

—"Oh, very interesting!" Enrique says. That conversation **reminds him**[7] that he needs to change euros to local money and he says "Lily, let's go to the bank please, I need to exchange euros for Panamanian currency."

—"No problem!" Lily responds and adds, "You know that here in Panama you can use the **balboa**[8] or the dollar. A balboa is worth the same as a dollar because we have an international banking system."

She smiles and continues driving. On the way Enrique sees many small stores with local products. He also sees lots of construction, because the Government of Panama is building a metro system.

---

6 **copper** - cobre, elemento químico
7 **reminds him** – le recuerda
8 **Panama's official currency** - el balboa

6 — Panama City

Enrique and Lily continue their tour, and he observes everything with great attention. They go along the *Corredor Sur*, which is a **highway**[1] that goes over the water in the Bay of Panama. Enrique can see *Panama La Vieja* and modern Panama City.

Then they enter Panama City through the ***Cinta Costera***[2] and drive-by *Avenida Balboa*. In the city, there are many **skyscrapers**[3] and Enrique sees a very large statue and asks, "Tell me Lily, who is the person on the monument?"

—Lily responds, "That is the statue of Vasco Núñez de Balboa. He was one of the Spanish explorers of the 1500s and

---

1 **highway** - autopista
2 **Cinta Costera** - Coastal Beltway
3 **skyscrapers** - rascacielos

that's why our currency is called the Balboa. He was the first Spaniard to see the Pacific Ocean from here."

—"Wow, what an interesting story!" Enrique says.

In a few minutes, Enrique admires the beautiful *Cerro Ancón* hill where a giant flag of Panama flies. On the slopes of the hill is Casco Viejo. It is the old original Colonial city and the Pacific entrance to the Panama Canal. Lily is still driving her *Uber*, and they enter a very large bridge, she points with her hand.

—"Enrique, we are now on the *Puente de las America's* over the Panama Canal. This bridge connects North America with South America. The Panama Canal is a very important waterway that connects the Pacific Ocean with the Atlantic Ocean. The Canal is very important for the world economy because of its strategic location."

Enrique is surprised and tries to take pictures of everything around him with his smartphone, —"**I don't want to forget**[4] any of this, Lily. I really like Panama, and I have been here for only two hours," Enrique smiles. "I'm so excited!"

They continue talking, he asks about the city, and they also talk about their schools. Lily says that she will graduate from high school this year too.

Enrique is impressed that Lily is so young to drive an *Uber* and asks:

---

4 **I don´t want to forget** – No quiero olvidar

—"Hey Lily, you are very young. At your age, are you allowed to drive an *Uber* car?"

—"Yes, here in Panama, I can drive with a special permit during the day until 9:00 p.m.," Lily says. "I drive to take visitors from the airport to *El Valle*."

—"Lily, you are really brave to drive in this traffic!" — Enrique says with a **chuckle**[5].

—"No, I'm not brave at all, my friends think I'm a little crazy, ha ha! What I like the most is that when I drive, I get to meet a lot of people and I also earn some money for college. This is just temporary."

Enrique talks more about his life in Spain, his friend Beto and also that they will graduate from high school this year. They

---

5 **chuckle** – risa baja y entre dientes

talk some more while she makes a quick stop at the bank for Enrique to change his money.

They are already close to the family's house. Enrique is excited and curious because he wants to know more about the place where he will be living for the next few weeks.

—"Lily, **I am eager**[6] to learn more about this country, its culture, and you, my host family!"

Finally[7], after almost one hour, they arrive at a small hotel in a valley. Enrique **is a little surprised**[8] and does not understand.... Why doesn't Lily take him to a house? Why are they stopping in a place that doesn't look like a normal house?

---

6 **I am eager** - tengo muchas ganas
7 **Finally** - finalmente
8 **is a little surprised** – está un poco sorprendido

7 — An Inn

Lily and her family live in a house that is also **an inn**[1]. They are the **owners**[2] of the inn, because it is a family business. Enrique just found out that he is going to live in an inn, which is very interesting for him. The parents are Mr. Danilo and Mrs. Rosa. The hostess and boss of the inn is Mrs. Rosa, that's why the inn is called La Posada de Rosa. The inn is located in *El Valle de Antón*. The inn is a hotel, but smaller. Travelers and tourists like to visit it because it is **cheaper than a**[3] hotel and provides a friendlier experience.

Mrs. Rosa is very happy to finally meet Enrique in person. Enrique thinks that Rosa and Lily are special names because they

---

1 **an inn** - un hostal
2 **owners** - dueños
3 **cheaper than a** – más barato que

are names of flowers. Mrs. Rosa **meets**[4] Enrique and is very happy.

—"Welcome Enrique! I'm Rosa, your host mother."

—"Hello! Thank you very much! Nice to meet you, Mrs. Rosa."

—"Just call me, Rosa, please!" She hugs him immediately and continues talking, "I hope that you enjoyed the *Uber* ride and the Panama traffic from the airport, ha ha!"

—"Yes! I enjoyed it very much, Rosa. Thank you!" Enrique says.

—"Enrique, this is my dad, Danilo Tapir," Lily says.

—"Nice to meet you, Mr. Danilo," Enrique says and **shakes his hand**[5].

—"Nice to meet you, young man. Please call me Danilo. Welcome to *El Valle!*"

—"Thank you very much, Danilo!"

—"**Don't mention it**[6]**,** Enrique!"

—"I'm so happy to finally be here with you!"

Enrique wants to be nice, but he feels very tired from the trip. Mrs. Rosa gives him the key to the room where he is going to stay and also gives him the Wi-Fi password on a piece of paper. The key has a **key ring**[7] made of wood with the number eight on it. Enrique doesn't think much about it, but he does think it's a coincidence that the room is number eight, like his birthday, and his lucky number.

In his room, Enrique sees a tourist brochure with a QR code to listen to a podcast. He uses his smartphone with an international

---

4 **s/he meets** – él/ella conoce
5 **shake hands** - le da la mano
6 **don't mention it** - estamos a la orden
7 **key ring** - llavero

signal to scan the code. On the website, he can see information about the area where the inn is located and thinks it is a wonderful place. He listens to an audio about *El Valle de Antón*, but Enrique is very tired, so he falls asleep listening to the audio.

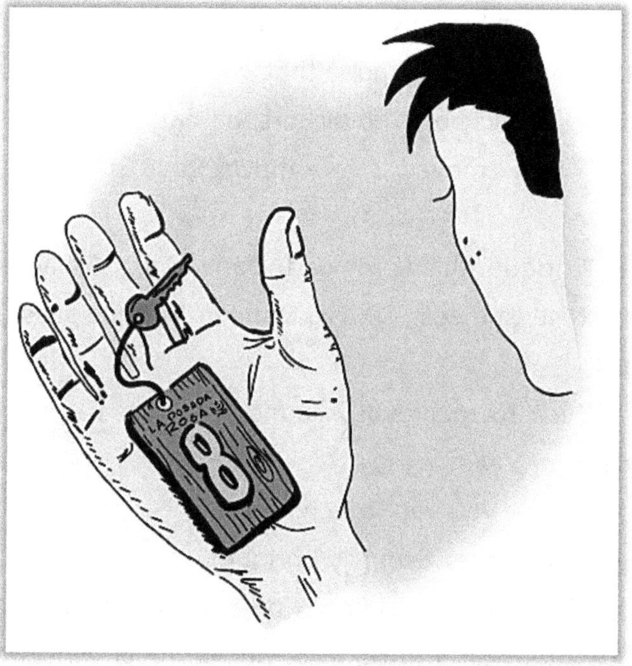

8 — The Panamanian Breakfast, Delicious!

It is Saturday morning. Enrique **wakes up**[1], takes a shower, and feels full of energy. He goes to the dining room to have breakfast. He has the opportunity to talk to Mrs. Rosa, Lily, Mr. Danilo, and other people who are at the inn.

—"Good morning, Rosa! How are you today?"

—"Good Enrique! I am doing well. Did you sleep well?"

—"Yes, I always sleep well when I'm very tired, ha ha!"

—"I imagine you did because your trip from Spain to Panama is very long. There are seven-hours of difference."

Mr. Danilo waves while he eats his ***carimañolas***[2] and drinks his black coffee.

—"Good morning, Enrique! Please sit down at our table."

Enrique sits down and begins to eat breakfast. He doesn't know what he's eating, but he thinks it's all very delicious and exclaims:

1**wakes up** – se despierta
2 **carimañolas** – frituras hechas de puré de yuca que se rellena con pollo, carne de res o queso antes de ser fritas

—"What is this I'm eating? It's very delicious. Is it an empanada or a stuffed potato?"

—"It's a *carimañola* made with yucca dough and stuffed with ground meat!" Mrs. Rosa smiles and explains, while Lily smiles.

—"Thank you for the explanation, yummy! They are delicious! I really like *carimañolas,*" Enrique says as he enjoys the new flavors and smiles.

Enrique eats five *carimañolas*, coffee, and fresh cheese. He is very hungry! He eats and continues talking to Mrs. Rosa and the people at the table.

—"Rosa, I learned about Panama and some legends in my Latin American history class. I also listened to a *podcast* about this valley. There is a legend about the mountain and the crater of a volcano that I want to know more about."

—"Oh, yes! Of course, Enrique," Mrs. Rosa says, there are several legends. Danilo knows the legends very well, and he is always ready to tell them. Danilo knows the history of the Indigenous tribes in Panama because he is a native of *El Valle* and his family is a descendant of an Indigenous chief.

—"Of course!" Mr. Danilo assures and begins to tell the legend of *Flor del Aire*. "This story was told to me by my **great-grandfather**[3] like this..."

---

3 **great-grandfather** - bisabuelo

9 — The Legend of *Cacique Urracá* and *Flor del Aire*

—"*Many years ago in a place in the 'New World' that is now Panama,*" Mr. Danilo says, "*There was an Indigenous tribe. This tribe still exists, they are very hard-working people with very beautiful and intelligent women. When the Spanish arrived, the Indigenous chief was* **Cacique**[1] *Urracá, the most courageous warrior who fought against the European explorers in the lands of Panama.*

The Cacique had a beautiful daughter" —Mr. Danilo continues—, "*Princess Flor del Aire, who was engaged to be married to Yaraví who was a young, strong Indigenous warrior. But sadly, the princess had no love for him, because she was in love with a Spaniard.*

Yaraví, realizing that Flor del Aire did not feel love for him, suffered greatly, and in his despair, he **jumped**[2] *from the mountain, where he lost his life.* **After that**[3], *Flor del Aire promised*

---

1 **Cacique** – indigenous chief
2 **jumped** - saltó
3 **After that** – Después de eso

*to forget her Spanish love and started crying and **wandering**[4] around the forest for a long time. One day, Flor del Aire fell asleep crying on the top of the mountain on the green grass. Feeling sorry for her, the mountain covered her with a **blanket**[5] of vegetation, and as a result immortalized her. That is how her silhouette has remained visible as a great symbol of her love. Many people believe in the legend and say that Yaraví is the sleeping volcano. Experts also claim that the valley is the crater of a dormant volcano with small hills and rocks."*

—"Wow! Danilo, that's an **amazing**[6] legend, but too romantic for me," Enrique says. "I don't like romanticism, I like hiking, ha ha! I want you to tell me more about the volcano, please. Where is it?"

Mr. Danilo is not very impressed with Enrique's reaction and does not smile.

—"No, Enrique, it is not 100% romantic. When you get a chance to walk the trails, immerse yourself in the springs, and climb the mountain, you will understand its meaning much better."

Enrique is a little **embarrassed**[7] with Mr. Danilo because he thinks he doesn't take the story seriously and he says:

—"I'm sorry, Danilo! I promise I will respect the history and legends of Panama because I want to learn more about this country, okay!"

—"To answer your last question," Mr. Danilo adds, "the volcano is **under**[8] our feet. *El Valle de Antón* is the crater of a dormant volcano."

---

4 **wandering** - vagando
5 **blanket** - manta
6 **amazing** - asombrosa
7 **embarrassed** - avergonzado
8 **under** – debajo

Enrique is amazed and **eagerly**[9] wants to know more about *El Valle de Antón* and its legends. Mr. Danilo gets up from the table and he says:

—"Well, another time we will talk more about this topic. It is already late and time to go to the market. We have to help prepare the open-air-market for tomorrow, Sunday." —Mr. Danilo adds, "Lily, remember that you have to go to the airport to pick up other tourists, please."

—"Yes, Dad," Lily says.

—"Enrique, if you want, you can come by the market later."

—"Okay Danilo!" Enrique says.

—"See you later!" Mr. Danilo responds as he says goodbye to everyone.

---

9 **eagerly** - con entusiasmo

10 — Enrique and Beto Communicate

Although Panama is a small country with a great variety of landscapes, such as the cordillera, which is a **paradise**[1] at more than 800 meters above **sea level**[2]. *El Valle* has a cool and pleasant climate. Panama also has beaches on two oceans.

The house of Beto's host family is on a beach called Costa Esmeralda. This beach is 30 minutes away from the inn where Enrique is staying.

As they promised to communicate with their cellular phones, Enrique writes a short text to Beto.

—"Hello Beto! Can you talk?"

—"Yes," Beto responds with a text and "ring ring!" his cellular phone rings immediately.

—"Hello, Beto! How are you?"

—"Hello, Enrique! I'm doing great, and you?"

—"I'm fine too," Enrique says. "**Though**[3] my host family is a little different because they don't live in a house. They live in an-inn."

---

1 **paradise** - paraíso
2 **sea level** - nivel del mar
3 **though** – aunque, sin embargo

—"Wow!" Beto says, "what a surprise, ha ha! My host family lives in a house on the beach on the Pacific Ocean side. The beach is called Costa Esmeralda."

—Enrique adds, "The strangest thing is that my family has an *Uber* driver who picked me up at the airport. Her name is Lily and she is the daughter of my host family. She is very smart and pretty. This place is called *El Valle de Antón*."

—"That´s so cool Enrique! Then we can take an *Uber* ride in Panama. Awesome! Today, Saturday I will be at the beach with my family, but I want to visit you in *El Valle* tomorrow, Sunday!" Beto says.

—"Great! The town has an open-air-market on Sundays. Many people visit this market to buy handicrafts and fresh products such as fruits and vegetables. I can ask Lily if she can drive her *Uber* to your house and bring you here. We can meet at the market here in *El Valle!*" Enrique says.

—"Good idea! You text me when Lily answers back. I will also share my GPS location," Beto says.

—"Yes, I will text Lily, and I will let you know her answer," Enrique says.

Enrique is very excited that he will probably see his friend Beto tomorrow. When he finishes his conversation with Beto, he texts Lily, and asks if she can pick up his friend Beto tomorrow.

— She texts back, "<u>yes</u>".

Immediately, Enrique texts Beto and confirms that Lily will pick him up in her Uber.

After that, Enrique goes to the Central Park market and helps Mr. Danilo and other **locals**[4] in *El Valle* to set up **tents**[5] for the Sunday market. Enrique works very late and falls asleep very tired.

---

4 **locals** - lugareños
5 **tents** - carpas

11 — The Boys Explore the Town

It is Sunday morning and Enrique wakes up, eats his breakfast, and talks to Mrs. Rosa and Mr. Danilo, and the people at the inn.

—"Where is Lily?" Enrique asks them.

—"She ate her breakfast early and left in her *Uber* to work and to pick up your friend Beto," Mr. Danilo answers.

—"Wow! She is a very good and punctual girl," Enrique says and smiles.

—"Yes, she is also a **hard-working**[1] girl," Mrs. Rosa says.

Enrique smiles and hopes with all his heart that he will be able to see Lily later. He also knows it is going to be a very good day because he is going to see his friend Beto. So he talks with other people at the inn about the weather and *El Valle*, and then he walks out to the local market.

As promised, Lily drops Beto in the Plaza and Lily goes to run errands with her mom. Enrique and Beto **get together**[2] in the

---

1 **hard-working** - trabajadora
2 **get together** - se reúnen

park at *Plaza del Parque Central*. They are very happy to see each other **again**[3]. They are curious to visit the market and learn more about the town of *El Valle.*

Enrique says:

—"Beto, you know this valley is also known as the place of the legend of the mountain of *La India Dormida.* Look at the mountain over there on the left, it is shaped like a woman who is asleep. The legend is very **sappy**[4], can you believe she died of love? Ha ha!"

—"Really Enrique? I think it's a very cool legend. We can visit the mountain; do you want to do some **hiking**[5]?"

—"Good idea, you know, some people also say that *El Valle* is a sleeping volcano. People believe the volcano is the brave Indigenous warrior who died for *La India Dormida.* There are also rumors that there are **goblins**[6] and ghosts on the trail."

Beto is curious to know more about the trail and asks Enrique, "How long do you think it will take us to climb the mountain?"

—"I don't know, but look there in the center of the park. There is a statue and a map. Let's go see!" Enrique answers.

In the center of the park, the boys look at the statue of the Indigenous princess *Flor del Aire*. The princess's face looks very familiar. It is almost the same as Lily's face, but they think it is a coincidence. They also look at and read the map of the town and *La India Dormida* Trail.

---

3 **again** – nuevamente, de nuevo
4 **sappy** - cursi
5 **hiking** - senderismo
6 **goblins** - duendes

Beto reads and tells Enrique, "Look here, it says *El Valle* has a museum and a small zoo. Popular activities are hiking the mountain trail, swimming in the natural hot and cold springs."

Enrique reads another section of the map and adds, "There are **square shaped trees**[7] and petroglyphs called *Piedra Pintada*. Also, *El Valle* is the home of the Panamanian **golden frogs**[8]."

The boys are excited about all the things they are going to learn about, and so they continue to walk around the market and learn about the local culture. They look for local food for lunch. They eat rice with chicken and drink ***chicheme***[9].

While talking about what they are going to do the next day, they walk and arrive at a park where there are many people playing dominoes. They see Mr. Danilo playing with several other people at a table.

Mr. Danilo greets them from a distance and says, "Come in closer, boys."

---

7 **square shaped trees** - árboles cuadrados
8 **golden frogs** - ranas doradas
9 **chicheme** - una bebida que se encuentra casi exclusivamente en Panamá hecha al hervir maíz dulce con canela, vainilla, leche y azúcar al gusto.

12 —The Dominoes Game at Parque de los Aburridos

Mr. Danilo goes to a park every Sunday with his friends after helping the townspeople with things for the local market. The *Parque de Los* **Aburridos**[1] is a famous park in Panama, but the truth is that it is not boring at all...

—"Enrique, Beto! Do you know how to play dominoes?" Mr. Danilo asks. Enrique and Beto look at him, but they **didn´t say anything**[2]. —"If you don't know how, you can learn here!" Mr. Danilo says.

They smile and sit at a table, and play for two hours, having fun and talking to local people. They drink coconut water, which they love coconut water because it is cold and refreshing. Not only that, but they also eat **empanadas**[3], and green mango salad with vinegar, salt and pepper.

Suddenly, Enrique receives a text from Lily. Enrique feels very happy, and his face gets very red. He replies to her with a short text.

Beto asks, "What's wrong, Enrique? Who is texting you? You look silly, and your face is red as a tomato."

---

1 **bored people** - aburridos
2 **didn´t say anything** - nada
3 **empanadas** - empanadas son discos de masa rellenos y cocinados fritos u horneados.

—"It's all right, Beto! It's Lily who wants to talk, maybe she's coming to play dominoes with us."

Beto says, "I don't think so Enrique, you're crazy! Lily has to work on her *Uber.*"

A few seconds later, Lily calls "ring, ring!"

—"Hello!" Enrique answers his phone.

—"Hello, Enrique! It's Lily, I'm near *El Valle*. Tell me, does Beto need to go back to the beach with his host family? If so, I can give him a ride."

—"Thanks Lily, but Beto is going to stay in *El Valle* tonight because tomorrow we are going hiking. We are going to visit the waterfalls and the *La India Dormida* trail."

—"That's great! Well then, I will see you tonight at the inn for dinner," Lily says.

—"Sounds perfect Lily, see you later," Enrique says.

—"Okay, bye **guys**[4]!" Lily says.

---

4 **guys** – chicos/chicas o ambos

13 — Dinner and Conversation

It is Sunday afternoon and time for dinner at *La Posada de Rosa*, and all the guests gather to eat. Today Mrs. Rosa cooks her famous **pork stew**[1], the house special with white rice, *plátanos maduros* and for dessert *Dulce Tres Leches*. The inn has a five-star rating on Google, which describes the stew as delicious.

Enrique and Beto arrive in the dining room and a little later Lily arrives and greets them. Beto greets Lily with two kisses on the cheeks and a hug, as it is done in Spain. Enrique on the other hand gets very nervous, his face turns red as a tomato again, and he doesn't know what to do, but Lily approaches him and greets him with a kiss on the cheek and a hug as it is done in Panama. It is very common in Latin America and Europe to greet with one or

---

1 **pork stew** - estofado de cerdo

two kisses and a hug when you see an acquaintance. Enrique's heart is beating very fast:

—"Hi Lily!! I'm so glad you're already here," Enrique says excitedly.

—"Hi guys! What's up?" Lily says as she smiles.

—"Beto and I are here waiting for...! Well, waiting for the food! We are very hungry," —Enrique says with a chuckle.

—"Good thing you're hungry! Because today there is a delicious pork-stew. I'm going to the kitchen to help my mom. She is very busy," Lily says as she walks towards the kitchen.

Half an hour later..., Enrique, Beto, Lily, Mrs. Rosa, and Mr. Danilo sit down to enjoy the food. They talk happily about everything they saw in *El Valle*, when they arrived at the park and when they played dominoes. Then Enrique says:

—"Tomorrow, Beto and I are going hiking in the mountains. Do you have any recommendation for us?"

Mr. Danilo gives them important information.

—"Walking along the trail takes about four hours, you can see the *Piedra Pintada* and several **waterfalls**[2]. The waterfalls are called: ***Chorro***[3] *de Los Enamorados, Salto del Sapo, Chorro Escondido,* and *Chorro de La ***Moza***[4]."*

—"You can swim and cool off in the water," Lily adds. There is a lot of green vegetation and a wonderful view at more than 800 meters above sea level. It is also cold at the top.

—"Oh! and you have to bring a snack and water," Mrs. Rosa recommends, "...and there are snakes, so you have to wear sneakers or hiking boots, not **flip-flops**[5] or *Crocs*."

---

2 **waterfall** - cascada
3 **Chorro** – torrente de agua
4 **Moza** - término formal y antiguo para una joven doncella
5 **flip flops** - chancletas/chanclas

—"**Sounds exciting**[6]! It's going to be a lot of fun. Lily, are you coming with us?" Beto asks and looks at Enrique as Enrique smiles and his cheeks turn red.

Lily declines the invitation and says, "I like the idea, but I cannot go, tomorrow is my day off, and I have to **run errands**[7] with my mom. But I can go at the end of the day to see you at the exit of the trail."

Enrique replies, "Sorry you cannot come with us, but we will see you at the end of the trail. **Still**[8], it's going to be a great adventure for Beto and me."

Mr. Danilo gets up from the table and tells them:

—"Well guys, let's all go rest, tomorrow you have an adventurous day ahead of you, and you need all the energy to climb the mountain!"

—"Danilo is right, tomorrow you will need a lot of energy. Let's go to sleep!" Mrs. Rosa adds.

She goes to close the **gate**[9] of the inn's patio and exclaims:

---

6 **Sounds exciting** - suena emocionante
7 **to run errands** - hacer mandados
8 **Still** - Todavía
9 **gate** - portón

—"Oh how nice! It's raining and it's fantastic! Because it means we're going to have a cool night to sleep without hot temperatures. Also, tomorrow is going to be a comfortable day for you."

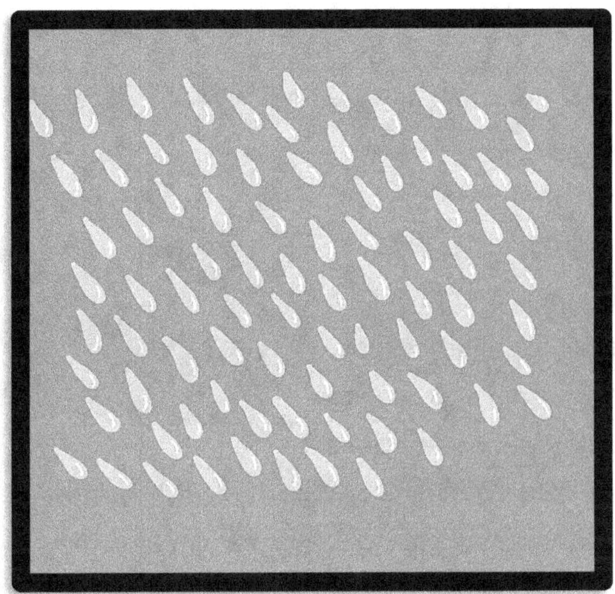

14 — Paper Map or GPS?

It's 6:00 a.m. in *El Valle de Antón* and nobody needs an alarm clock, because the roosters and hens get up when the sun rises and the roosters start crowing.

—"**¡Quiquiriquí! ¡Quiquiriquí!**[1]"

Enrique and Beto get up and get ready for their journey, they go to the dining room to have breakfast. Enrique drinks coffee with milk and Beto orange juice. They wear comfortable clothes sneakers, sunglasses, and hats. Also, they take water, cereal bars, and cellphones with GPS.

—"Good morning! Are you ready?" Lily asks them.

—"Ready!" answer Enrique and Beto. So Lily goes with them to the entrance of the mountain trail. At the entrance there are adults and children who are local guides for the visitors, they are wearing hats in the shapes of typical Panamanian animals such as: golden frogs, toucans, monkeys, **spiders**[2], horses, and tapirs. The man wearing the tapir hat looks familiar; in Panama, a tapir is a wild pig and is also known as a **macho de monte**[3]. Enrique approaches and sees that it is Mr. Danilo Tapir, now Enrique

---

1**¡Quiquiriquí! ¡Quiquiriquí!** - Onomatopeya o escritura en español para el sonido de un gallo. En inglés se escribe cock-a-doodle-do
2 **spiders** - arañas
3 **tapir or wild pig** - macho de monte

understands why Mr. Danilo knows the history of the mountain so well.

—"Hi guys, good morning and welcome to the trail of the India Dormida!" Mr. Danilo says.

—"What a surprise to see you here. Lily, why didn't you tell us that Danilo works here?" Enrique says with a surprised face.

—"Oh, it's just very normal, so **I** always **forget**[4] that detail," Lily answers.

—"No problem!" Enrique says.

Mr. Danilo offers them paper maps, but the boys don't take them, they think the GPS on their cellphones are enough.

At the entrance there is an Indigenous girl wearing a golden frog hat selling **handicrafts**[5] in the shape of small green and gold frogs made of ceramic. She also sells mangoes, coconut water, *platanitos*, coconut candies, and ***pepitas de marañón***[6].

Tourists buy handicrafts as souvenirs, and snacks for the trail. Enrique and Beto buy coconut candies, *platanitos*, and cold

---

4 **I forget** - se me olvida
5 **handicrafts** - artesanías
6 **cashew nuts** - pepitas de marañón

coconut water in bottles for their snacks. Other children are also wearing hats in the shape of animals offering to be **tour guides**[7], but Enrique replies:

—"No, thanks, kids! You guys are very nice, but we don't need tour guides, we have our GPS on our phones. We want to go alone to have our own adventure, thank you!"

----

7 **tourist guides** - guías turísticos

15 — The Trail and the Volcano

Enrique and Beto enter the trail, walk for thirty minutes and see the *Piedra Pintada* hieroglyphics. Some people think that it is an Indigenous map of *El Valle*. Also, they see a lady coming down with her shoes in her hand, her purse in the other hand to go to work. They greet her and continue walking up the mountain.

They walk for another thirty minutes and are amazed. The weather is cool because they are already in the forest of tall trees. There are also wild orchid flowers of many colors everywhere. This is the head and the "hair of *La India*" …

—"Look Beto! There are toucans over there on the right. Take a picture," Enrique says.

In the middle of the trees, they see a big **sloth bear**[1] moving very, very slowly.

—"Take more pictures, Beto! This is sensational!" Enrique says.

---

1 **sloth bear** - oso perezoso

—"But Enrique, you have to take pictures with your cellphone too, because my battery only has three bars, okay?"

—"Okay Beto!" Enrique says.

So under a very hot sun and cool wind, they follow the road and after 30 minutes more they arrive at the *Chorro de Los Enamorados*. The two boys are amazed.

Enrique shouts with excitement, "Beto, let's go for a swim! Quick, let's go into the waterfall. It looks cool!"

Enrique wants to swim, also he wants to take a selfie in that beautiful place. He takes his cellular phone out of his pocket, and it falls-out of his **sweaty hands**[2]. Enrique **quickly**[3] jumps into the water.

—"Oh no, no, no, no! My cellphone! It's soaked!!!"

—"Phew! How lucky" Beto assures, our cellphones are waterproof, as always, our mothers think of everything. If the phones get **soaked**[4] they won't get damaged, ha ha!

—"Yes, **that's lucky!**[5] Enrique says. **I hope**[6] it works well the rest of the way because we didn't take the paper map Danilo offered us.

---

2 **sweaty hands** - manos sudorosas
3 **quickly** - rápidamente
4 **they soaked** - se mojan
5 **that's lucky!** - ¡qué suerte!
6 **I hope** - Ojalá

They use Beto's cellular phone to take pictures and continue their adventure.

—"Yay!" Beto says and jumps into the water from the highest rock.

They swim for 15 minutes, get out of the water and dry off, and eat their snacks. They put into practice what they know about taking care of nature and put the garbage in their backpacks so as not to damage the trail's ecosystem. Then they get ready to continue walking.

They walk ten minutes more, go very carefully up another very **steep hill**[7] and arrive at the "**throat**"[8] of *La India*. From there, they enjoy the beautiful view of the crater of the sleeping volcano that forms *El Valle*.

They continue until they reach the **stone steps**[9] that are very high because they go up to the "**chest**"[10] of *La India*. When they reach the top, they can see some beautiful plants and aerial flowers like orchids, Panama´s national flower.

Suddenly, Enrique feels a mild tremor, as if the volcano is waking-up under their feet. Also... they hear screams.

—"Hello, hello, hello! Oh, my God! Hello, hello, hello!"

—"Is it a woman?" Enrique wonders.

---

7 **steep hill** - cerro muy empinado
8 **throat** - garganta
9 **stone steps** - escalera de piedra
10 **chest** - pecho

16 — The Voices

Enrique looks at Beto, they hear voices and shouts again "Hello, hello, hello!"

They worry, walk for two more minutes and see no one. They are already on the path by the "**waist**"[1] and the "**navel**"[2] of *La India* and then between the trees they see two big birds, two red, green, blue, and yellow **macaws**[3] that sing and talk.

—"Hello, hello, hello! Oh, my God! Ha ha ha!"

Enrique and Beto start laughing because the macaws **frightened them**[4] and are so funny.

—"Oh my goodness, I'm glad no one is in danger, and it's just those crazy birds, ha ha!" Beto says.

Enrique remembers that there are many myths about this mountain, plus there are **ghosts**[5] and elves. Enrique is a little scared, but continues walking and comments:

---

1 **waist** - cintura
2 **belly button** - ombligo
3 **macaws** - guacamayas
4 **frightened them** - los asustaron
5 **ghost** - fantasma

—"In the podcast I listened to, they mention the ghost of *Flor del Aire*."

—"How scary, Enrique! Shut up and don't say **silly things**[6]. We have to walk fast to get to the end of the trail, besides, it's very hot. I hope it rains!"

They continue walking and now the weather is a little windy. They see some boys **flying kites**[7]. Enrique and Beto say hello and stop to take pictures of the valley. They are already close to the *Chorro de La Moza*.

—"We have to hurry to *Chorro de La Moza* to take another quick dip in the water and take a **nap**[8]. Let's go fast, Enrique!"

As if by magic the weather gets cooler, there is a nice wind and the sun's rays **sparkle**[9] as a gift from Mother Nature. The boys reach the waterfall without any problems. Enrique and Beto are amazed:

—"Wow, Beto, this place is even more fascinating than

---

6 **silly things** - tonterías
7 **flying kites** - están volando cometas
8 **nap** - siesta
9 **sparkle** - brillan

the previous spring! It's a good place to make our *TikTok* #Panama"

—"Yes! Good idea, this is amazing. There is fresh water and thermal water coming out of the volcano. Let's go for a swim first, Yay! Wooohooo!!" Beto says.

This time, Enrique takes his cellular phone out of his pocket very carefully before entering the water to swim and looks at it, and sees a problem.

—"Oh, Beto, my cellphone isn´t working properly because it is wet after I drop it in the *Chorro de Los Enamorados*. My GPS isn´t working, either."

—"But Enrique, if our cellphones are waterproof, why isn't yours working?"

—"Yes, you're right, but the screen is broken, noooo!" Enrique exclaims.

—"Don't worry! Let me check my phone" Beto says. "Oh, oh! My battery is **almost dead**[10]. We have to take another selfie soon."

—"Okay, it's okay," Enrique says. "Don't worry, we have to enjoy this moment here."

Enrique and Beto sit on the **edge**[11] of the river talking quietly and want to take a nap; but again, they feel a mild tremor in the earth under their feet.

At first the air is calm, and then as if by magic, there is a fresh wind again. The boys notice the fragrance of flowers and watch the waters move. At the same time, they hear a very sweet voice speaking to them. They can see a beautiful woman in the water combing her shiny black hair, but in reality, it is a ghost that

---

10 **almost dead (battery)** - casi muerta
11 **edge** – orilla (del río)

looks very much like Lily. They cannot believe what they see, and Enrique says:

—"How strange! It cannot be Lily, she's with Mrs. Rosa..."

—"You're right..." Beto says in a frightened voice.

17 — The Ghost in the Spring

Enrique and Beto do not understand what is happening, because what they see is very beautiful and does not seem real. They are confused, but enchanted.

—"Hello!" She swims, and smiles as she speaks to them, "Thank you for coming to visit our trail and the mountain!"

—"Lily, is that you?" Beto asks.

—"No, I am not Lily. I am *Flor del Aire, La India Dormida*."

Enrique and Beto look at **each other**[1] in amazement without being able to speak, Enrique finds the courage to say:

—"*Flor del Aire*, are you *La India Dormida* of the Mountain? But you look like Lily."

---

1 **each other** – el uno al otro

Flor del Aire explains, "Yes, Lily, her father Danilo and I have the same native origin, that's why we **look alike**[2]. They also belong to the *Sociedad Secreta de La India Dormida* (SSID) and their mission is to attract visitors to the trail. Yaraví, my eternal lover, is now the sleeping volcano that causes the gentle tremors. It is very important that a volcano stays calm to **avoid**[3] the eruption of hot lava, for this reason it is very good for us when people who respect and appreciate our culture and history visit us."

—"Wow!" Enrique says.

—"¡Double wow!" Beto says.

Flor del Aire continues, "We need more people to visit the trail so that the Yaraví volcano does not feel so lonely, as visitors keep it happy and peaceful. SSID has the goal of taking care of the mountain to avoid **hate**[4] and harm. The Volcano on the other hand continues to admire my precious mountain, India Dormida."

—"That's all very important!" Enrique says.

—"Yes!" Beto assures.

—*Flor Del Aire* comments further, "Because of my loyalty to our tribe, the Gods allow me to come down from the mountain to this spring to talk to the travelers and dream that someday I will see my love, Carlos Dominguez. He was a Spanish explorer."

—Enrique says, "Dominguez? How fascinating, that's my last name, and I'm from Spain. My ancestor who came to America in the 1500s was named Carlos Dominguez."

Flor del Aire says "Enrique, you are a descendant of Carlos! That's why destiny brought you to Panama, what joy I feel in my heart!!"

---

2 **look alike** - parecerse
3 **avoid** - evitar
4 **hate** - odio

Enrique thinks about all the things that happened to him since his arrival in Panama, and now he understands better... he remembers the lucky penny in the parking lot and the energy he felt when he touched it... he also remembers the number eight as his birthday and what he felt when his teacher told them about the exchange trip to Panama. It all makes sense now!

Beto on the other hand feels frightened and opens his big eyes and asks, "Miss *Flor del Aire*, what do you want from us? How can we help you?"

Flor del Aire answers, "**you have helped a lot**[5] by respecting our culture and taking care of nature, by not littering our village, *El Valle* and the trail. The spirits of our ancestors are very appreciative of your actions to maintain peace between the races."

Suddenly, the scent of flowers is stronger, and *Flor del Aire* disappears as if by magic. Enrique and Beto look at each other like crazy, unable to believe what they saw. They cannot believe it and think, did they really see *Flor del Aire* or was it all part of a vision?

It gets dark, and their cellular phone batteries are almost dead. They cannot believe what happened. They take their things, put on their sneakers and walk very quickly.

—"I hope we are not lost, next time we need to bring a paper map," Beto comments.

They reach the end of the trail and suddenly see Lily in the distance. They look at each other and wonder, is it Lily or is it *La India Dormida* again?

—"Lily! Lily! It's you, we're so happy to see you," Enrique says. You're going to think we're crazy, but we saw a vision.

—"What are you guys talking about?" Lily smiles.

---

5 **you have helped a lot** - han ayudado mucho

—"At first we thought it was you," Beto says.

—"Oh no! Sorry guys," Lily **laughs**[6].

—"Don't laugh Lily, at first we felt a little panic, we thought it was you, and then we thought it was a ghost...but then we knew it was a vision of *La India Dormida*," Enrique says.

—"Ufff! Don't panic guys. *Flor del Aire* is the cheerful spirit and the guardian of the mountain who is very respectful and proud of her tribe. Many local people are secret members of the SSID. I am one of them myself, we help take care of the mountain. We need more people who want to be part of the society, because we are working to reforest the mountain. If you come up with a good idea, you are welcome to be part of the society."

—"This is all very interesting. I'm interested in helping SSID, I will think about it," Enrique replies. "My family in Spain has a sunflower farm."

—"This is all very exciting, but it's darkening. After this adventure, I'm very tired and very hungry. Shall we continue talking on the way home?" Beto asks.

Enrique and Beto return with Lily to the inn. They have dinner together and talk about their experiences on the trail and the mountain. When they

---

6 **laughs** - ríe

finish dinner, the boys and Lily dance like macaws for a *TikTok* #Panama challenge.

After that, Lily takes Beto in her *Uber* back to his host family's house on the beach.

The rest of the week, the boys **spend more time**[7] with their host families and get to know the culture and traditions of Panama better.

Beto takes lots of pictures of places, plants and animals that are new to him. He also tastes different types of local food, and a variety of new fruits and vegetables.

Enrique spends much of his time studying the traditions and legends of *La India Dormida*. He talks to various people in the area, takes notes in his notebook and writes down his plans to help the local community.

Two weeks have passed, and the boys are going back to Spain in a few days. It is time to prepare for their airplane trip.

---

7 **spend more time** – pasar (más) tiempo

18 — See You Soon!

The day arrives to return to Spain. Lily drives Enrique to the airport while they enjoy a long conversation in the car. Next, Beto arrives with his host family. Beto says goodbye to his family and walks towards Enrique and Lily; they stop for a moment, greet each other and talk a little more. Beto is as always, a little nervous about boarding the airplane...

—"Well Lily, we have to say goodbye!" Enrique says in a sad voice.

—"I will see you soon, Enrique!" Lily says. "Remember that next summer I'm going to Spain."

—"Yes, guys, it's okay! We will see each other soon!" Beto says nervously. "Now, at this moment, I'm worried about traveling by airplane again!"

Enrique says, "Beto, this is the last part of our adventure in Panama. Everything is going to be okay!"

The three of them give each other a big hug and say goodbye. They know they will be together again in Spain next summer.

Enrique and Lily look at each other in the eyes and smile. Enrique's face doesn´t turn red like a tomato, but he feels a little nervous. They share their contact information on social media and promise to keep in touch. Lily is very enthusiastic to go to Spain.

—"Once again Lily, thanks to you and your parents for being so kind with me," Enrique says. "I really enjoyed Panama and want to come back and visit in the future again. I love everything about Panama."

—"I loved everything too, especially the food! I'm hungry again! Ha ha! Well, see you soon Lily," Beto says.

Happy, Enrique and Beto enter the giant airplane that is going to take them to Spain.

19 — Back to Spain with a Sustainable Plan

After a long trip, the boys arrive in Spain. At the airport, they hug, say goodbye, and go home with their parents.

At Enrique's house, his mother prepares a delicious dinner. They all sit down to eat and talk about the trip. Enrique's father looks at him and says:

—"Enrique, tell us more about your adventure in Panama."

Enrique tells them the details about *El Valle*, *La India Dormida* Mountain, their hiking trip, its history, the Sunday market and the experience at *La Posada de Rosa Inn*. He also tells them about Lily, her family and the vision of *Flor del Aire* that he saw on mountain.

—"Mom and Dad! You're going to think I'm crazy, but the most interesting part of this trip was literally the vision! A VISION!"

—"What are you saying, Enrique?" the mother asks.

—"When Beto and I walked along the trail, we saw a vision of the spirit of *La India Dormida* of the mountain. Right there at that moment, I knew about the main reason why I visited Panama," Enrique continues speaking with enthusiasm. "Now I have a great idea for my graduation project. It is about agriculture and natural resources because I already know what I want to study at the university! I want to be an agronomist engineer!"

—"Excellent!" comments the father. We really like that you came back from your trip so enthusiastic, so your trip was everything you wanted it to be and more. Now tell us more about your idea for the project, **we are all ears**[1].

Enrique explains his idea to help SSID with the reforestation of the mountain.

—"The idea is that for my graduation Capstone project I am going to make an ecological **proposal**[2] for *El Valle* and *La India Dormida* Mountain, but I am going to need your help. I want to be part of the *Sociedad Secreta de La India Dormida* (SSID) to work in the preservation of the mountain."

—"Enrique, that's a great idea!" his father assures.

—"How do you plan to do it?" the mother asks.

Enrique continues talking "First, with Lily's help I am going to join the Society (SSID) as a member. My idea is to organize the community to reforest *La India Dormida* Mountain with Panamanian sunflowers. Panamanian sunflowers are not an invasive species. Second, with the Society I will organize the **harvesting**[3] of the sunflowers to sell, or to extract oil and seeds. They can also sell the flowers and products at the Sunday open-market."

---

1 **we are all ears** - somos todo oído.
2 **proposal** – propuesta con una idea de proyecto.
3 **harvesting** - cosecha

The father says, "Wonderful idea Enrique, in time this project will help the people of the town because it can be a strong industry for the future of the community."

The mother exclaims, "I think your idea is great. You need to present the project to your teacher soon."

Then the father shares some very important historical and family information.

—"You know Enrique, the original sunflower seeds that started our business came from Latin America. Our ancestor Carlos Dominguez met an Indigenous girl on one of his exploration trips. She showed him the fields of sunflowers, and he brought the seed back to Spain as a transplant gift. I believe the girl was from Panama."

—"What a coincidence!" Enrique smiles and exclaims.

—"Destiny is really crazy, isn't it? Destiny took you to Panama to find out a little more about sunflowers, wow!" the father assures.

—"Enrique we are proud of you because you are interested in learning about your family's history. Also, your encouragement to reforest the land is a great idea. We want to support you in your idea for the project," the mother says.

—"Yes! Double Wow! Now it all makes more sense!" Enrique says with a happy face. "Especially because reforestation helps the mountain, the Indigenous people, and the people of the village. Mom and Dad, you are examples of **kindness**[4]. I am very proud of our family."

---

4 **kindness** - bondad

Enrique and his parents smile and continue eating. At the end of dinner, Enrique looks at his cellular phone and says:

"I am going to contact Lily and SSID to start with the ecological proposal. First, I'm going to start on social media with the #Panama #girasolestiktok #indiadormida. Also, when Lily visits us next summer, you guys will meet her. I know you will love her; she is a pretty, nice, and intelligent girl, ha!"

The end?

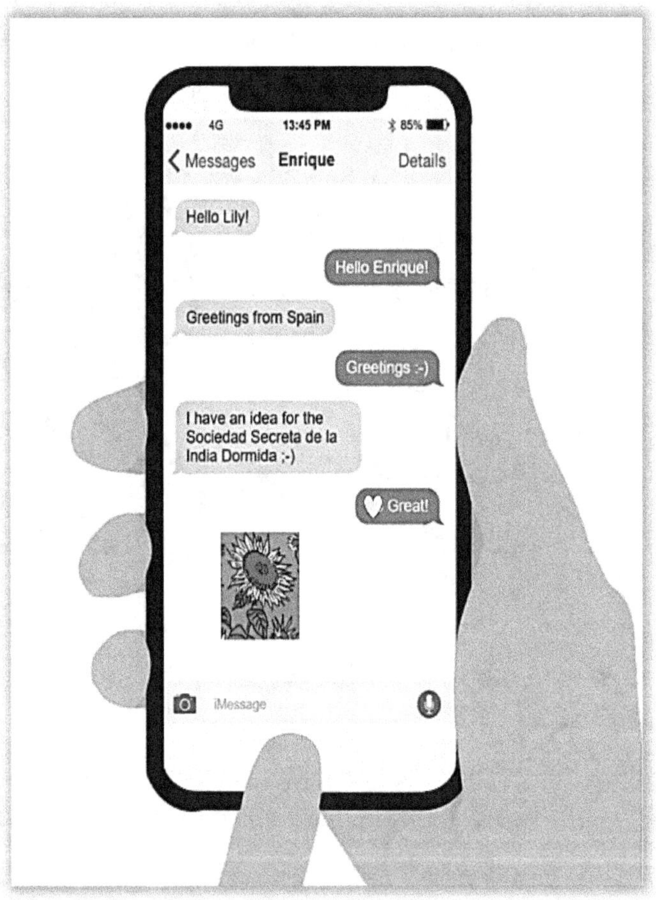

Glossary

English Words Predicted

Level: B1/B2

*Common European Framework of Reference for Languages
Text Analyzer - Find the CEFR level of texts from RoadtoGrammar.com

Intermediate Level 5-6

*International English Language Testing System

Unique word count: 1702

Number of words: 9356

Average sentence length: 10 words

A

a/an - un(a)/uno(s)
able - poder
about - acerca de
above - encima
accept - aceptar
acquaintance - conocido
actions - acciones,
activities - actividades
adds - agrega
admire - admirar
admires - él/ella admira
adults - adultos
adventure(s) - aventura(s)
adventurous – aventurero
aerial - aéreo
afraid - asustado
after(that)-después (de eso)
afternoon - tarde
again - de nuevo
against - en contra
age - edad
agricultura - agricultura
agronomist - agrónomo
ahead - adelante
air - aire
airplane - avión
airport - aeropuerto
alarm - alarma
alike - similar
all - todo/ todos
allow/allowed - permitir/permitido
almost - casi
alone - solo
along - a lo largo de
alongside - junto a

already – ya
also - además
although - a pesar de que
always - siempre
amazed - asombrado
amazement - asombro
amazing - increíble
America - América
American - americano
among - entre
ancestor(s) - ancestro(s) /antepasado(s)
and – y
animals - animales
answer(s) - respuesta(s)
any - ninguna
anything - cualquier cosa
appears - aparece
appreciate(s) - aprecio
appreciative - agradecido
approaches - se acerca/se aproxima
April - abril
are - ellos(as) son
área - zona/área
around - alrededor
arrival - llegada
arrive(d) - llegar/llegaron
arrives - él/ella llega
as – como
ask(s) preguntar, él/ella pregunta
asleep - dormido
assures - asegura
at - a
ate – él/ella comió
athletic - atlético
Atlantic - Atlántico
atended - asistió
attention - atención
attentive - atento
attract - atraer
audio - audio
August - agosto
avenida- avenida
avoid - evitar
away - fuera
awesome - increíble

B
back - espalda
backpacks - mochilas

balboa, Panamanian currency - balboa, moneda panameña
bank - banco
banking - bancario
bars - barras
battery(ies) - batería(s)
bay - bahía
be - ser
beach(es) - playa(s)
beats - late
beautiful -hermosa
because -porque
before - antes de
begins - él/ella comienza
being - ser
believe - creer
bell - campana
belong - pertenecer
besides - además
best/better – lo mejor/mejor
between - entre
BFF - mejor amigo(a) por siempre
big - grande
birds - aves
birthday - cumpleaños
black - negro
blanket - manta
blue - azul
boarding - embarque, abordaje
boat - bote
body - cuerpo
boots- botas
bored/boring - aburrido/aburrido
boss - jefe
both - ambos
bottles - botellas
boy(s) - niño(s)
brave - valiente
breakfast - desayuno
bridge - puente
bring - traer
brochure - folleto
broken - roto
brought - trajo
building - edificio
business - negocio
busy - ocupado
but - pero
buy - comprar
by - por

bye! - ¡adiós!

C

cacique – indigenous chief
call(s) - llamar /él,ella llama
called - llamado
calm - calma
came - llegó
can/cannot - poder/no poder
canal - canal
candies - dulces
Capstone Project - Proyecto final
car(s) - carro/coche(s)
care - cuidado
carefully - con cuidado
carimañolas - frituras hechas de puré de yuca
Casco Viejo - Ciudad colonial en Panamá
Catholic - católico
causes - causas
center - centrar
central - central
ceramic - cerámico
cereal - cereal
Cerro Ancón hill - Cerro Ancón
challenge - desafío, reto
chance - el chance/ la oportunidad
change - cambiar
chaperones - chaperones/acompañantes
person - persona
cheaper - más económico/barato
check - cheque
cheek(s) - la(s) mejilla(s)
cheerful - alegre
cheese - queso
chest - pecho
chicheme - una bebida de maíz dulce
chicken - pollo
chief – jefe(a)
children - niños
chuckle – risa baja y entre dientes
Cinta Costera - Coastal Beltway
city(ies) - ciudad(s)
claim - afirmar
class(es) - clase(s)
climate - clima
climatic - climático
climb - escalada
clock - reloj
close - cerrar

closer - más cerca
clothes - ropa
coasts - costas
coconut - coco
code - código
coffee - café
coin – moneda
coincidence -coincidencia
cold - frío
college - universidad
colonial - de los tiempos coloniales
colonization -colonización
colors - colores
combing - peinando
come up - sube
comfortable - cómodo
coming - viniendo
comment(s)- comentario(s)
common - común
communicate -comunicar
community - comunidad
complete -completo
confirms - confirma
confused - confundido
connection - conexión
connects - conecta
construction - construcción
contact/ed - contacto /contactado
continent - continente
continue(s) - seguir, continúa
conversation - conversación
cooks - cocineros
cool off - refrescarse
cool! - ¡genial!
cooler - más frío
coordinate - coordinar
copper - cobre, mineral
cordillera - cordillera, cadena montañosa
Corredor Sur autopista del sur
costera - costera
country(ies) - país(es)
countryside - campo, interior
couple - pareja
courage - coraje,valentía
courageous - valiente
course - curso
covered - cubierto
cráter - cráter
crazy - loco
create - crear

Crocs - Calzado de la marca Crocs
crowd - multitud
crowing – cacareo
crying - llanto
cultivate - cultivar
culture/cultural - cultura/cultural
curious - curioso
currency, money - moneda, dinero
cut - cortar

D
dad - padre
daily - a diario
damage - daño
damaged -estropeado
dance - danza
danger - peligro
dark - oscuro
data - datos
daughter - hija
day off - día libre
day(s) - dias)
dead - muerto
December - diciembre
declines – él/ella declina
delicious - delicioso
descendant(s)- descendientes)
describes - describe
design - diseño
despair - desesperación
dessert - postre
destiny - destino
detail(s)- detalle(s)
died - fallecido
difference - diferencia
different - diferente
dining - comida
dinner - cena
dip - aderezo
disappears – él/ella desaparece
distance - distancia
distributes – él/ella distribuye
do/did - hacer/hizo
does/doesn't - hace/no hace
doing - haciendo
dollar - dólar
dominoes - dominó
don't//didn't - no // no
done - hecho
door - puerta

dormant – latente
double - doble
dough - masa
down - abajo
dream - sueño
drinks - bebidas
drinks - él/ella bebe
drive - conducir
driver - conductor
drives - conduce
driving - conduciendo
drops - gotas
dry - seco
dry off - secar
Duke - Duque
Dulce Tres Leches (dessert) - Dulce Tres Leches (postre)
during - durante

E
each - cada
eagerly - con entusiasmo
early - temprano
earn - ganar
ears - orejas
earth - tierra
easy - fácil
eat/eats, eating - comer/ él/ella come, comiendo
ecological - ecológico
economy - economía
ecosystem - ecosistema
edge - borde
eight - ocho
either - cualquiera
elves - elfos
embarrassed - avergonzado
empanada(s) - empanadas son discos de masa rellenos y cocidos fritos u horneados.
enchanted - encantada
encouragement - ánimo
end - fin
energy - energía
engaged - comprometido
engineer - ingeniero
engineering - ingeniería
English - inglés
enjoy(ed) - disfrutar/disfruté
enjoys - él/ella disfruta

enough - suficiente
enter - ingresar
entering - entrando
enthusiasm - entusiasmo
enthusiastic - entusiasta
entrance - entrada
entrepreneurship - emprendimiento
eruption - erupción
especially -especialmente
established - establecido
eternal - eterno
Europe - Europa
European - europeo
euros – moneda europea
even - incluso
every/everyone - todos/todos
everything - todo
everywhere - en todas partes
examples - ejemplos
excellent - excelente
exchange - intercambio
excited/excitedly - emocionado
excitement - emoción
excites - emociona, anima
exclaims - exclama
exists - existe
exit - salida
experience(s) - experiencia(s)
experts - expertos
explains - explica
explanation - explicación
exploration - exploración
explore - explorar
explorer(s) - explorador(es)
extract - extraer
eyes - ojos

F
face - rostro
falls out – caerse
familiar - familiar, conocido(a)
family(ies) - familia(s)
famous - famoso
fantastic - fantástico
farm - granja
fascinating - fascinante
fast - rápido
father - padre
favorite - favorito
feel(s) - él/ella siente, ellos/ellas sienten

feeling - sentimiento
feet - pies
fell asleep - se quedó dormida
felt - él/ella sintió
few - pocos
field(s) - los campo(s)
finally - por fin
find - encontrar
finds - él/ella encuentra
fine - multa
finish(es) – terminar, él/ella termina
first - primero
five - cinco
flag - bandera
flavors - sabores
flies - moscas
flight(s) - vuelo(s)
flip flops - chancletas, chanclas
flower(s) - flor(s)
flyer - volantes
flying - volador
follow - seguir
food - comida
for - por
forest - bosque
forever - para siempre
forget - olvidar
forms - eso forma
fought - luchó
found - encontró
found out - averiguado
four - cuatro
fragrance - fragancia
fresh – nuevo
friend(s) - amigo(s)
friendlier - más amigable
frightened - aterrado
frog(s) - rana(s)
from - desde
fruits - frutas
full - completo, lleno
fun/funny - divertido/a
further - más lejos
future – futuro

G

game(s) - juego(s)
garbage - basura
gate - portón
gather - recolectar

get(s)/got – ob/tener// él/ella ob/tiene, ob/tuvo
gets very red – se sonroja
gets up - se levanta
ghost(s) - fantasma(s)
giant - gigante
gift – regalo
girl(s) – niña(s), chica(s), muchacha(s)
give(s) – dar, él/ella da
glad - contento
go/goes-ir/voy/va/vamos
goal - meta
goblins - duendes
god(s) – Dios(es)
going - yendo
gold - oro
golden - dorado
good - bien
goodbye – adios
goodness - bondad
government - gobierno
GPS - (por sus siglas en inglés) Sistema de Posicionamiento Global
grade - grado - escolar
graduate (will) - graduan/graduarán
graduation - graduación
grandfather - abuelo
grass - hierba, grama, pasto
great - genial
greatly - muy
green - verde
greet(s) - saludar/saluda
ground - suelo
groups - grupos
guardian - guardián(a)
guests - huéspedes
guides - guías
guys - los chicos(as)
ha ha! - ja ja! onomatopeya para reír
had - tener/tenía
hair - cabello
half - medio
hand(s) - mano(s)
handicrafts - artesanías, manualidades
handsome - guapo
happened, happening- sucedió, sucediendo
happily, happy - felizmente, feliz, contento
hard - duro

harm - dañar
harvesting - cosecha
hat(s) - sombreros
hate - odio
have, has – tener, él/ella tiene
having - teniendo
he, him, his - él (pronombre), él (objeto de pron.), su (posesivo)
head - cabeza
hear - oír
heart - corazón
heart beating –latiendo (corazón)
Hello! Hi! - ¡Hola! ¡Hola!
help, helped, helping - ayudar, ayudar, ayudar
helps - él/ella ayuda
hens - gallinas
here - aquí
Hey! - ¡Oye!
Hieroglyphics - jeroglíficos
high, highest - alto, más alto
highway - autopista
hiking - senderismo
hill(s) – colina(s), sierra(s)
historical - histórico
history - historia
home - casa
hope, hopes, I hope that - esperar
Ojalá(que) – esperar/desear que
horses - caballos
hospitable - hospitalario
host(ess) - anfitrión(a)
hot - caliente
hotel - hotel
hour(s) - hora(s)
house - casa
how - como, cómo
hug(s) - abrazo(s)
huge - enorme
humid - húmedo
hundred, one hundred - centenas, cien
hungry - hambriento
hurry - apurarse

I
I - yo
I am - Yo soy/ yo estoy
I am eager to... - Tengo ganas de...
I have - yo tengo

I have been here for only... - Solo he estado aquí ...
I imagine - yo imagino
I will - voy a
I will/I´ll - Yo haré
Idea - idea
immediate, immediately - inmediato, de inmediato
immerse yourself – sumergirte
immortalized- inmortalizado
important – importante
impressed- impresionado
improve - mejorar
in, into - en, en
India Dormida - Nombre propio de la montaña en Panamá.
India – indigenous, india, amerindia, indígena
industry - industria
information -información
inn - posada, hostal
innovation - innovación
instead - en lugar de
intelligent - inteligente
interest, interested - interés, interesado
interesting - interesante
international- internacional
Internet - Internet
introduce - introducir
invasive invasor
invitation - invitación
is - él/ella es
isn't - él/ella no es
isthmus – istmo es una estrecha franja de tierra que une dos más grandes.
it - eso
It looks cool! - ¡Se ve genial!
it's, its - es, su

J
join - unirse
journey - viaje
joy - alegría
juice – jugo
jumped él/ella saltó
jumps   él/ella salta
just - solo

K
keep - guardar

key - clave
kids - niños
kilometers - kilómetros
kind, kindness - amable, amabilidad
king - rey
kiss(es) - beso(s)
kitchen - cocina
know, he/she knows, knew - saber, él / ella sabe, supo
known - conocido

L
lady - dama
land - tierra
landowner - terrateniente
lands - tierras
landscapes - paisajes
large - grande
last - último
late - tarde
later - luego
laugh - reír
laughing - risa
laughs - él/ella se ríe
lava - lava (volcán)
leader - líder
learn, learns - él/ella aprende, ellos/ellas aprenden
learned - él/ella aprendió
learning - aprendiendo
leave - abandonar
left - izquierda, solo quedan
legend(s) - leyenda(s)
less - menos
lesson - lección
let - dejar
let's - vamos
level - nivel
life - la vida
like (verb) /like (similar) - gustar (verbo) / parecerse (similar)
likes - a él/ella le gusta
listen, listens, listened - escucha, él/ella escucha, escuchado
listening - escuchando
listens - escucha
literally - literalmente
littering - tirar basura
little - pequeño, poco
live, lives - vivir, él/ella vive

living - viviendo
local - local
local people, locals - gente local, lugareños
located - situado
location - localización
logo - logo
lonely - solitario
long - largo
look(s) like - parece
looking - buscando
looks - él/ella mira
lost - perdió
lot(s) - lote(s)
love, loves, loved - amor, él/ella ama, amado
lover - amante
loyalty - lealtad
luck, lucky - suerte, afortunado
lunch - comida

M
macaws - guacamayos, guacamayas
made - hecho
magic - magia
main - principal
mainland - continente
maintain - mantener
make, makes - hacer, él/ella hace
man - hombre
mango (oes) - mango(s)
many - muchos
many years ago - hace muchos años
map(s) - mapa(s)
March - marzo
market - mercado
married - casado
mathematics - matemáticas
maybe - quizás
me, tell me - me (objeto de pronombre), dime
meaning - significado, sentido
means - eso significa
meat - carne
media - medios de comunicación
meet(s) - reunir, conocer, él/ella conoce
member(s) - miembro(s)
mention - mencionar
met - reunió
meters - metros

metro - metro, modo de transportación
middle - medio
mild - suave, ligero
miles - millas
milk - leche
minutes - minutos
miss - extranar
mission - misión
mobile(s) - móvil(es)
modern - moderno
mom - mamá
moment - momento
money - dinero
monkeys - monos
monte - monte, montaña
monument – monumento
more - más
morning - mañana
most - la mayoría
mother(s) - madre(s)
mountain(s) – montaña(s)
move, moving - moverse, moviendo
moza - término formal y antiguo para
una joven doncella
Mr., Mrs., Miss - señor, señora, señorita
much - mucho
museum - museo
my - mi
myself - yo mismo
myths - mitos

N
name(s) - nombre(s)
named - llamado
nap - siesta
narrow - angosta
national - nacional
native - nativo
natural, nature - natural, naturaleza
navel - ombligo
near - cerca
need, needs - necesitar, él/ella necesita,
necesidad
nervous - nervioso
nervously - nerviosamente
never - nunca
new - nuevo
next - próximo
nice - bonito
nice people - gente amable

nickname - apodo
night - noche
no, not - no, no
noble - noble, aristócrata
nobody - nadie
noise - ruido
nor - ni
normal - normal
north - norte
notebook - cuaderno, libreta
notes - notas
notice(s) - aviso(s)
November - noviembre
now - ahora
number - número
numerous - numeroso

O
observes - él/ella observa
obvious - obvio
ocean(s) - océano(s)
of - de
offering - ofrecimiento
offers, offered - él/ella ofrece, ofreció
Oh - Oh
oil - aceite
okay - okey
old, oldest - viejo, más viejo o antiguo
on - en
once - una vez
one - uno
only - solamente
open-market - mercado abierto
opens - él/ella abre
opportunity - oportunidad
or - o
orange - naranja
orchid(s) - orquídea(s)
organize - organizar
origin, original - origen, original
other/another - otro/otra
our - nuestro(a)
out - afuera
outdoor - exterior
over - sobre
overwhelmed - abrumado
own - propio
owners - propietarios

P

Pacific - Pacífico
pack - paquete
Panama La Vieja - La ciudad antigua de Panamá
panamanian - panameño
panic - pánico
paper - papel
paradise - paraíso
parents - padres
park - parque
parking - estacionamiento
parque - parque
part - parte
passed - aprobado
password - clave, palabra secreta
path - sendero, camino
patio - patio
peace - paz
peaceful - tranquilo
penny(ies) - centavo(s)
people - gente
pepper - pimienta
perfect - perfecto
permit - permiso
person - persona
petroglyphs - petroglifos
Phew! - ¡Uf! sign of relief
phone(s), cellular phone, cellphone - teléfono(s), teléfono celular, teléfono celular
pick up - recoger
picked up - recogido
picture(s) - foto(s)
piece - trozo
Piedra Pintada - Piedra Pintada o painted stone
pig - cerdo
place(s) - lugare(s)
plan(s) - plan(s)
plants - plantas
plátanos maduros - plátanos maduros
play soccer - jugar fútbol
play video games - jugar video juegos
played - jugó
playing - jugando
plaza - plaza
pleasant - agradable
please - por favor
plenty - mucho

plus - más
pocket - bolsillo
podcast - pódcast
points - puntos
popular - popular
pork - cerdo
posada - posada
possibility - posibilidad
potato - patata, papa
practice - práctica
precious - precioso
prepare, prepares - preparar, él/ella prepara
present - regalo, presente
preservation - preservación
pretty - bonita
previous - anterior
princess - princesa
probably - probablemente
problem(s) - problemas)
products - productos
program - programa
project(s) - proyecto(s)
promise, promised - promesa, prometida
properly – apropiadamente, adecuadamente
proposal - propuesta
proud - orgulloso
provides - proporciona
puente - puente
punctual - puntual
purse - bolso
put(s) - poner, él/ella pone

Q

Queen - Reina
question - pregunta
¡Quiquiriquí! - Onomatopeya para el sonido de un gallo.
quick, quickly - rápido rápidamente
quietly - en silencio

R

races - razas
rains, rainy, raining - lluvias, lluvioso, lloviendo
rating - clasificación
rays - rayos
reach - alcanzar
reaction - reacción

read, reads - lee, él/ella lee
ready - listo
real, reality, really - real, realidad, de verdad
realizing - dándose cuenta
reason - razón
receives, received - él/ella recibe, recibió
recommendation - recomendación
recommends - él/ella recomienda
red - rojo
reforest, reforestation - repoblación forestal, reforestar
refreshing - refrescante
region - región
relieved - aliviado
remain - permanecer, mantener
remained - se mantuvo
remember(s) - recuerda, le recuerda
reminds him, reminds them - le recuerda, les recuerda
RENFE - The National Network of Spanish Railways, it has High Speed (AVE) trains. - RENFE – abreviatura para Red Nacional de Ferrocarriles Españoles, cuenta con trenes de Alta Velocidad (AVE)
resisted – resistido, él/ella resitió
resources - recursos
respect - respeto
respectful - respetuoso
respecting - respecto a
respond, responds - responde, él/ella responde
rest - descanso
result - resultado
return - regresar
rice - arroz
ride - montar
right - derecho
ring(s) - anillo(s)
rises - sube
river - río
road - la carretera
rock(s) - roca(s)
romantic, romanticism - romantico, romanticismo
room - habitación
roosters - gallos
rumors - rumores
run errands - hacer recados, diligencias

S

sad, sadly - triste, tristemente
said - dijeron
salad - ensalada
salt - sal
salto - salto
same - mismo
sappy - cursi
Saturday - sábado
saw - vi, viste, vio, vimos, vieron
say, says, saying - decir, él/ella dice, diciendo
scan - escanear
scared - asustado
scary - de miedo
scent - olor
school(s) - escuela(s)
science - ciencia
screams - gritos y carcajadas
screen - pantalla
sea(s) - mar (es)
search - búsqueda
season(s) - temporada(s), estación(es)
second(s) - segundos)
secret - secreto
secreta - secreta
section - sección
seed(s) - semilla(s)
seem - parecer
sees - él/ella ve
selfie - foto selfi
sell, sells, selling - vender, él/ella vende, vendiendo
sensational - sensacional
sense - sentido
separated - apartado
seriously - seriamente
set - colocar
seven - siete
several - varios
shakes - sacudidas, temblores
shall - deberá
shape, shaped - forma, con forma de
share, shares - compartir, él/ella comparte
she, her, hers - ella (pronombre), ella (objeto de pron.), su (posesivo)
she's - ella es
shiny - brillante
shoes - zapatos

short - corto, pequeño
should - debería
shout, shouts - gritar, él/ella grita
showed - él/ella presentó
shut up - cállate
side - lado
sign - letrero
signal - señal
silhouette - silueta
silly - tonto
since - ya que
sing - canta
sit, sits - sentarse, se sienta
skyscrapers - rascacielos
sleep, sleeping - dormir, durmiendo, dormido(a)
slopes - pendientes, falda, ladera
sloth bear - oso perezoso
slowly - despacio
small, smaller - pequeño, más pequeño
smart - inteligente
smartphone(s) -teléfono(s) inteligente(s)
smile(s) - sonrisa(s)
snack(s) - merienda(s)
snakes - serpientes, culebras
sneakers - zapatillas, zapatos deportivos, tenis
so - asi que
soaked - mojado
soccer - fútbol
social - social
society - sociedad
solutions - soluciones
some - algunos
someday - algún día
soon - pronto
sorry - lo siento
Sounds exciting! - ¡Suena emocionante!
Sounds perfect - Suena perfecto
south - Sur
souvenirs - souvenirs
Spain - España
Spaniard - español, la ciudadanía
Spanish - español, el idioma
sparkle - brillar
speak, speaks, speaking - hablar, él/ella habla, hablando
special - especial
species - especies
spend (more) time – pasar (más) tiempo

spiders - arañas
spirit(s) - espíritu)
spring(s) - nacimientos de aguas
square - cuadrado
star - estrella
start, started - empezar, empezo
stay, stays, staying - quedarse, él/ella quedarse, quedando
steep - empinado
steps - pasos
stew - estofado
sticker - pegatina
still - todavía
stone - roca
stop, stopping - parar, detener, parando
store - tienda
story - historia
strange, strangest - extraño, mas extraño
strategic - estratégico
strong, stronger - fuerte, más fuerte
student(s) - estudiantes)
study, studying - estudiar, estudiando
stuffed - relleno (a)
such - tal
suddenly - de repente, repentinamente
suffered - sufrió
suitcases - maletas
summer - verano
sun - sol
Sunday(s) - domingo(s)
sunflower(s) - girasol(s)
sunglasses - gafas de sol
sunlight - luz de sol
super - súper
support- apoyo
surprise, surprised - sorpresa, sorprendido
sustainable - sostenible
sweaty - sudoroso
sweet - dulce
swim, swims - nadar, él/ella nada
swimming - natación
symbol - símbolo
system - sistema

T

table - mesa
take, taking - tomar, tomando
taken - tomado

takes - él/ella toma, lleva
takes a shower - ducha
takes out - saca
tales - cuentos
talk, talks, talking - hablar, él/ella habla, hablando
talked (I, she) - hablé, habló
tall- alto
tapir or wild pig - tapir o jabalí - macho de monte
tastes - sabores
teacher(s) - maestro(a)(s)
tell, tells - decir, él/ella dice
temperatura(s) – temperatura(s)
temporary -temporal
ten - diez
tents - carpas
text(s) - texto(s)
texting - mensajes de texto
tan - que
thank, thanks - gracias
that, those - que, aquellos
the - la
their - sus
them, themselves - ellos, ellos mismos
then - luego
there are - existen
there is, there are - hay, hay
thermal - térmico
they - ellos
thing(s) - cosa(s)
think, thinks - pensar, él/ella piensa
thirty - treinta
this, these - este, estos
those - esos
though - sin embargo
thought - pensamiento
three - tres
throat - garganta
through - mediante
Tik Tok - Tik Tok red social
time - tiempo
time off - tiempo libre
tired - cansado
title - título
to - para
today - hoy
together - juntos
told - dijo
tomato - tomate

tomorrow - mañana
tonight - esta noche
too - también
took - tomó
top - cima
top it off - por si fuera poco
topic - tema
toucans - tucanes
touch, touches – tocar, él/ella toca
touched - tocó
tour - gira
tourism - turismo
tourist(s) - turista(s)
towards - hacia
town - ciudad, pueblo
townspeople - gente del pueblo
traditions - tradiciones
traffic - tráfico
trails - caminos
train - tren
transplant - trasplante
travel, traveled - yo viajo, viajé //él/ella viaja, viajó
travelers - viajeros
traveling - viajando
tres - árboles
tremor(s) - temblor(es)
tres - tres
tribe(s) - tribu(s)
tries - él/ella trata
trip(s) - viaje(s), excursione(s)
tropical - tropical
truth - verdad
turn, turns - girar, él/ella gira
two - dos
types - tipos
typical - típico

U
Uber - Transportation company with an app
Uff! - ¡Uff! sonido de alivio
unable - incapaz
under - bajo
understand, understands - entender, él/ella entiende
universo - universo
university - Universidad
until - hasta
unusual - raro

up - arriba
use, uses, used - uso, él/ella usa, usado
usually - generalmente

V
valley - valle
variety - variedad
various - varios
vegetables - verduras
vegetation - vegetación
very - muy
video - video
view - vista
village - pueblo
vinegar - vinagre
visible - visible
visión - visión
visit, visits - visitar, él/ella visita
visited(I) - visité(yo)
visitors - visitantes
voice(s) - voz(s)
volcano - volcán

W
waist - cintura
waiting- esperando
wakes, waking - despierta, despertando
walk, walks, walking - caminar, él/ella camina, caminando
walked (I) - caminé
walks up (he) - camina hacia (él)
wandering - vagando
want, wants, you wanted- querer, él/ella quiere, quisiste
warrior - guerrero
was - fue
watch - ver
water(s) - agua(s)
waterfall(s) - cascada(s)
waterproof - impermeable
waterway - canal navegable
waves - saluda con las manos
way - via
we, us - nosotros
wear, wearing - llevar, llevando
weather - tiempo
website - sitio web
week(s), weekend(s) - semana(s), fin (es) de semana(s)
welcome - bienvenidos

well - bien
what - qué
when - cuándo
where - donde, dónde
which - cuales, cuáles
while - mientras
White - blanco
who - quien, quién
whose - de quien, cuyo
why - por qué
wild - salvaje
will - voluntad
wind, windy - viento, ventoso
with, without - con, sin
woman, women - mujer, mujeres
won't - no lo haré
wonder - preguntarse
wonderful - maravilloso
wonders - maravillas
wood - madera
Wooohooo! - ¡Wooohooo!
work, works, working - trabajar, él/ella trabaja, trabajando
world – mundo
worry, worried - preocuparse, preocupado
worth - valor
would - haría
Wow! - ¡Guau!
Writes - él/ella escribe
wrong - equivocado

Y Z
yay! - Hurra!
year - año
yellow - amarillo
yes - sí
you - tú
you're - estás
young - joven
your, yours - tus tuyo
yucca - yuca
yummy - delicioso
zoo – zoológico

About the Author

Nayka Barrios Jaén, also known as Señora Miller, is a Panamanian-American author. She is also a Spanish instructor. Nayka graduated from the *Instituto Nacional de Panamá*, she has a Business Degree from the *Universidad del Istmo, Panamá;* has a Master's Degree in Applied Linguistics from the *Universidad de Jaén, Andalucía, España*. She also holds a Postgraduate Certificate in Higher Education from Harvard University, USA.

Nayka was born in *Panamá* and used to spend summers with her *abuela Frede* in *Bejuco* which is a village near *El Valle* and *La India Dormida* Mountain, where the legend and the story take place. Nayka is passionate about her native *Panamá*, and the Spanish language preservation. As an educator she is also enthusiastic about teaching young generations to respect other cultures and to protect the environment through sustainable initiatives.